Picture Perfect

~➤ Book Six ➤~

DISNEP PRESS
New York

Illustrated by the Disney Storybook Artists
Designed by Deborah Boone

Printed in China

First Edition
1 3 5 7 9 10 8 6 4 2

Library of Congress Catalog Card Number on file.

ISBN 978-1-4231-2921-9
F904-9088-1-10140

For more Disney Press fun,
visit www.disneybooks.com

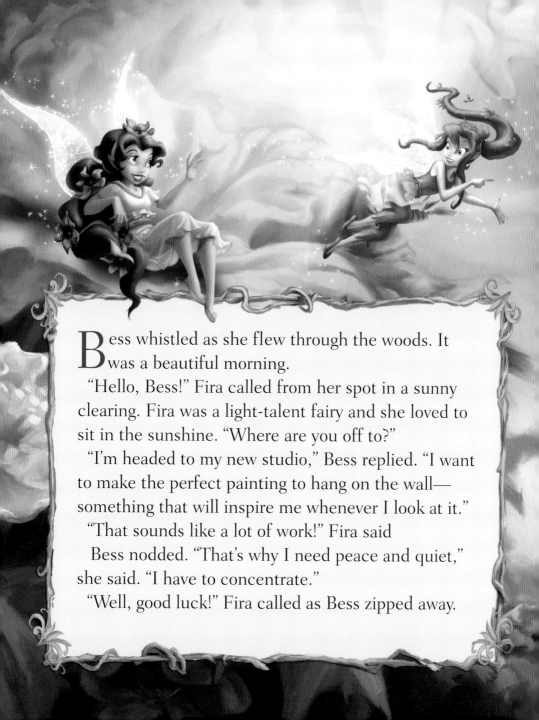

Bess whistled as she flew through the woods. It was a beautiful morning.

"Hello, Bess!" Fira called from her spot in a sunny clearing. Fira was a light-talent fairy and she loved to sit in the sunshine. "Where are you off to?"

"I'm headed to my new studio," Bess replied. "I want to make the perfect painting to hang on the wall— something that will inspire me whenever I look at it."

"That sounds like a lot of work!" Fira said

Bess nodded. "That's why I need peace and quiet," she said. "I have to concentrate."

"Well, good luck!" Fira called as Bess zipped away.

Fira settled back, basking in the sun.

"Where is Bess going?" someone asked.

Fira opened one eye. "Oh, hello, Rani!" she said. "Bess is off to her new art studio. She said she needs some inspiration."

"Bess isn't feeling inspired?" Rani asked. She looked concerned.

"She is, but—" Fira started to explain.

But Rani wasn't listening. "I know just what she needs!" she said excitedly. "See you later, Fira!" With that, she hurried off toward Havendish Stream.

"It's *perfect!*" Rani cried as she plucked a smooth stone from the bottom of Havendish Stream.

"What's perfect?" Tinker Bell asked, flying up beside her.

Rani grinned at her friend. "This!" she exclaimed, holding out the stone. "Fira says that Bess needs some inspiration," Rani told Tink. "And I thought, what's more inspiring than a beautiful stone? I can't wait for Bess to see it!" With a wave, she hurried off.

"Inspiration, hmm?" Tink murmured to herself. Personally, whenever she needed inspiration, she just looked at the pots in her workshop. "That's it!" Tink cried. "I know just what Bess needs."

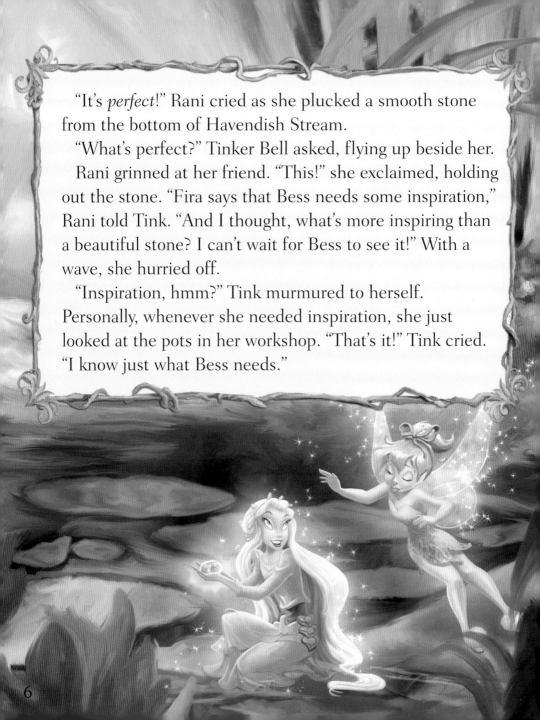

6

Moments later, Tink was on her way to Bess's workshop. She struggled to carry a large copper pot.

"Let me help you, Tink," Lily said. "Where are you taking this pot?"

Tink explained that she was taking the pot to Bess to give her some inspiration.

"Inspiration?" Lily said. "Wait! I need to go back to my garden. My violets are very inspiring!"

Tink grumbled a little as she and Lily flew back to the violet patch. Lily took her time selecting the perfect one. Then the two fairies dug up the flower and planted it in Tink's pot.

"Perfect!" Lily cried.

Tink had to agree that the pot and the flower were very inspiring. Even though the pot was a little more inspiring, in her opinion.

"Tink! Lily!" Beck called from a nearby tree branch where she was sitting with one of her squirrel friends. "Where are you going with that pretty flower and that beautiful pot?"

"Hi, Beck!" Lily cried as they flew past. "We're taking this to Bess!"

"Sorry we can't stop to talk," Tink shouted. "But she needs some inspiration right away!"

"Did you hear that?" Beck asked the squirrel. "Bess is feeling uninspired."

The squirrel chattered something.

"Hmm—" Beck replied, tugging thoughtfully on a strand of hair. "Now, I'm not saying that a walnut isn't inspiring," she said carefully. "But I had something else in mind."

Meanwhile, Bess had arrived in the deepest part of the woods. "There it is!" she sang as her brand-new art studio came into view.

Bess's studio was a plain wooden crate that had once been used to hold tangerines. Bess had found it washed up on the shore of Never Land. She had used magic to move it to a very quiet, peaceful part of the woods.

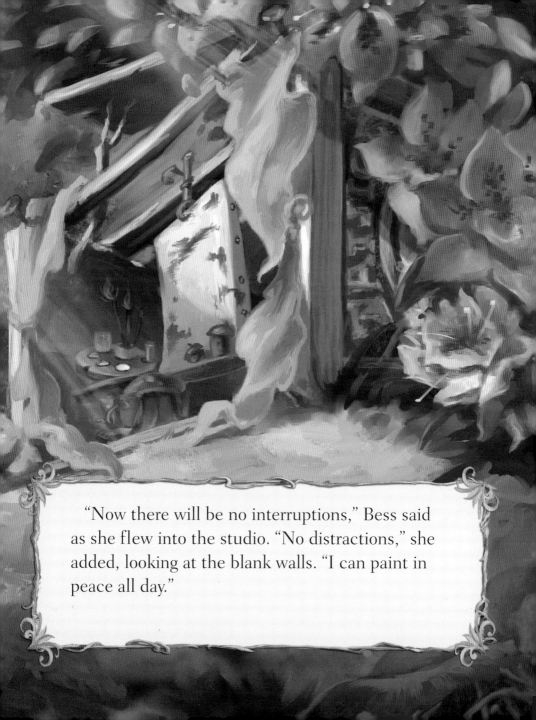

"Now there will be no interruptions," Bess said as she flew into the studio. "No distractions," she added, looking at the blank walls. "I can paint in peace all day."

Bess sat down at her stool and stared at the white birch-bark paper. She held up her paintbrush and got ready to make the first stroke. . . . But she couldn't decide what to paint.

That's odd, Bess said to herself. Usually, her mind was overflowing with ideas for beautiful paintings. But today, her mind was blank.

Should I paint a flower? she asked herself. *Or a tree? Or maybe a sunset? Hmm—* All of those things sounded pretty, but none of them seemed quite right. *I need something very special for my wall,* Bess told herself. *Something perfect. But what?*

Bess frowned at her easel. *Why aren't I feeling inspired?* she wondered, sighing heavily.

Above her, the leaves rustled in the breeze. Bess scowled up at them. "Shh!" she told them. "I need peace and quiet."

A bird chirped from a nearby branch.

Bess sighed.

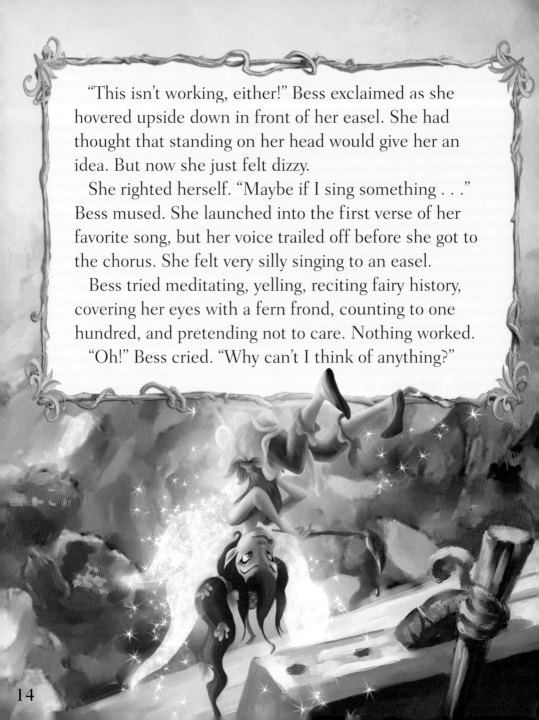

"This isn't working, either!" Bess exclaimed as she hovered upside down in front of her easel. She had thought that standing on her head would give her an idea. But now she just felt dizzy.

She righted herself. "Maybe if I sing something . . ." Bess mused. She launched into the first verse of her favorite song, but her voice trailed off before she got to the chorus. She felt very silly singing to an easel.

Bess tried meditating, yelling, reciting fairy history, covering her eyes with a fern frond, counting to one hundred, and pretending not to care. Nothing worked.

"Oh!" Bess cried. "Why can't I think of anything?"

Finally, Bess fell flat on her back. She stared up at the
ceiling of her studio. "I'm not going to move until I get an
idea," she said. "I mean it. I don't care how long it takes."

"*Knock, knock!*" someone said.

Bess turned her head.

A face peeked into the studio. "It's me, Fira! I wanted to
see how your painting was going. Why are you lying on the
floor? Are you hurt?"

"No, I'm fine, I was just thinking about what to paint."

Fira flew around the wall and landed inside the studio. "You haven't started yet?" she asked.

"Well," said Bess, "it's not that easy, you know. You can't just . . . start painting. You have to think about it first."

"But I've seen you *just start* painting a hundred times," Fira pointed out.

"Say," Beck replied, a bit desperately. "Isn't it time for your weekly light-talent meeting? Goodness, I bet it is. I'll just see you out." Bess hustled the confused Fira out of her studio.

"Hello, down there!" cried a friendly voice. Bess looked up to see Tink and Lily hovering overhead.

"We brought you a present," Lily said. She and Tink fluttered to a soft landing beside Bess. "It's from both of us," Lily explained.

"The pot's from me," Tink added.

"It's a beautiful pot," Bess said. "The flower is beautiful, too." She really meant it.

Unfortunately, what Bess needed was an idea for a painting, not a pot with a flower in it.

At that moment, there was a rustling from the underbrush. Beck and Rani stepped out of the woods.

Bess was starting to feel annoyed. How on earth would she ever get an idea with all of these distractions?

"I've brought you a present!" Rani said. She held out her river stone. "For inspiration."

"I brought something, too!" Beck said shyly. She held out two halves of a speckled red eggshell. "You can use these to mix paints in," she added.

"Thanks." Bess accepted the gifts. *Grr!* she thought. These gifts are wonderful. But honestly, I wish they all would just go away. How can I work surrounded by so many—"That's it!" Bess cried suddenly.

Grabbing her largest brush, Bess darted over to the long wall of her studio and started to paint. The other fairies watched, amazed, as a painting began to appear.

Finally, just as the sun was dipping below the trees, Bess stood back to look at her work. On the wall she had painted her five friends—all of them smiling. Bess smiled back at them. She was satisfied at last.

"What a beautiful picture!" Lily said.

"I like the way you put our presents in the background," Beck added.

"The pot looks especially nice," Tinker Bell pointed out.

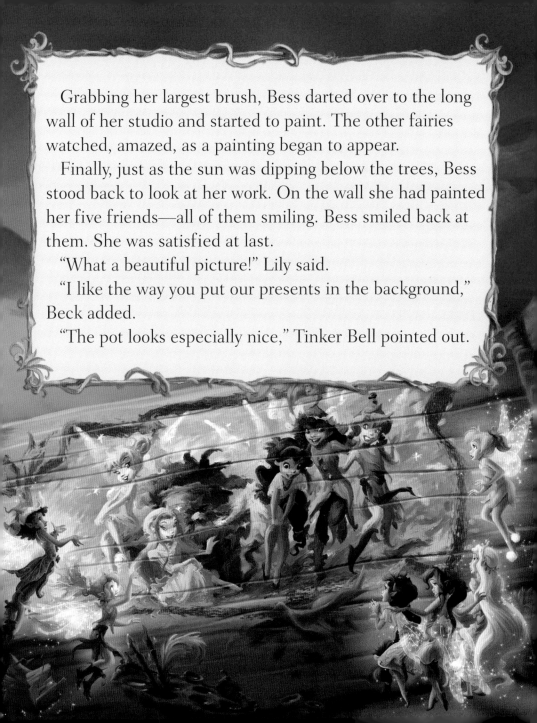

Bess put one arm around Fira and the other around Rani and grinned. "Now, if that isn't an inspired painting," she said to her friends, "I don't know what is."